I Am Smart, I Am Blessed, I Can Do ANYTHING!

BY Alissa Holder & Zulekha Holder-Young   ILLUSTRATED BY Nneka Myers

FLAMINGO BOOKS

FLAMINGO BOOKS
An imprint of Penguin Random House LLC, New York

First published in the United States of America by Flamingo Books,
an imprint of Penguin Random House LLC, 2020

Visit us online at penguinrandomhouse.com.

LIBRARY OF CONGRESS CATALOGING-IN-PUBLICATION DATA IS AVAILABLE.

ISBN 9780593206607

Manufactured in China

1 3 5 7 9 10 8 6 4 2

Design by Opal Roengchai
Text set in Gill Sans Alt One Book
This art was rendered in Procreate for iPad and Photoshop with lots of love!

Ayaan, you have made an impact on so many lives.
I created this affirmation for you and Alaïa to use in times of self-doubt.
It is my hope that you both always remember that you are smart,
you are blessed, and you can do ANYTHING!
—A. H.

For Amari, Amir, and Aria.
May you always know the power of your words,
and know that you are capable of anything you put your mind to.
Be positive in your thoughts, your words, and your actions always.
Thank you for continuing to inspire me.
—Z. H. Y.

For my family and close friends who believe in me every day!
—N. M.

AYAAN woke up bright and early.
He usually loved going to school.
But today he felt a little bit worried.

"Ayaan, where's your happy face?"
his mom asked.
"I'm not feeling so happy today."

"Sometimes at school I don't feel very smart.
I feel worried I won't know the answers."

Ayaan's mom looked into his eyes.

"Do you remember what we always say?"

He nodded.

"Let's say it together."

"I am smart."

"Let's say it louder now."

"I AM SMART!" they both shouted toward the sky.

Ayaan felt better, but deep down he was not so sure.

Outside, Ayaan took his mom's hand.
"Look who it is!" she said.
It was Mr. Grandpa. He waved and gave
Ayaan his usual morning greeting.
"Go get 'em, Ayaan! Today's going to be
a great day."

"Thanks, Mr. Grandpa,"
Ayaan replied quietly, but
deep down he wasn't so sure.

"Ayaan, Coco wants to
say good morning!"
Ayaan scratched the
little dog's ear like
he did every morning.
Coco wagged her tail.

Ayaan high-fived his
friend Amarli.
She lived just around
the corner.
"See you at recess,
Ayaan!" yelled his friend.

Ayaan was still quiet. His mom
squeezed his hand.
"Isn't it nice you have so many
wonderful people in your life?
People who care about you!

"What do we always say?
Let's say it together."
"I am blessed."
"Let's say it louder."
"I AM BLESSED!"
they both shouted.
Ayaan's mom picked him
up and swung him around.

Ayaan couldn't help
but giggle.

After they crossed the street,
Ayaan stopped to tie his shoe.
He had been practicing, but still
he asked his mom for help.
His mom replied, "I think today
is the day. Give it a try."
Ayaan concentrated on his shoe.

It took him a few minutes, but he tied his laces into a perfect bow.

"See, Ayaan! You can do anything.
Let's say it together."
Ayaan smiled. "I can do anything."
He looked at his mom.
"Louder?" he asked.
She nodded.
"I CAN DO ANYTHING!"
they both said together.

Ayaan let go of his
mom's hand, and she
bent down to give
him a big hug.

Ayaan was definitely starting to feel better.
Today was already becoming a good day.

He thought about what his mom had said.
He repeated those words to himself slowly
as he walked up the steps.
"I am smart, I am blessed,
I can do anything."

As he stood at the door to
his school, Ayaan said it again . . .

. . . this time out loud.

"I am smart,

I am blessed . . ."